Ghosts in the House!

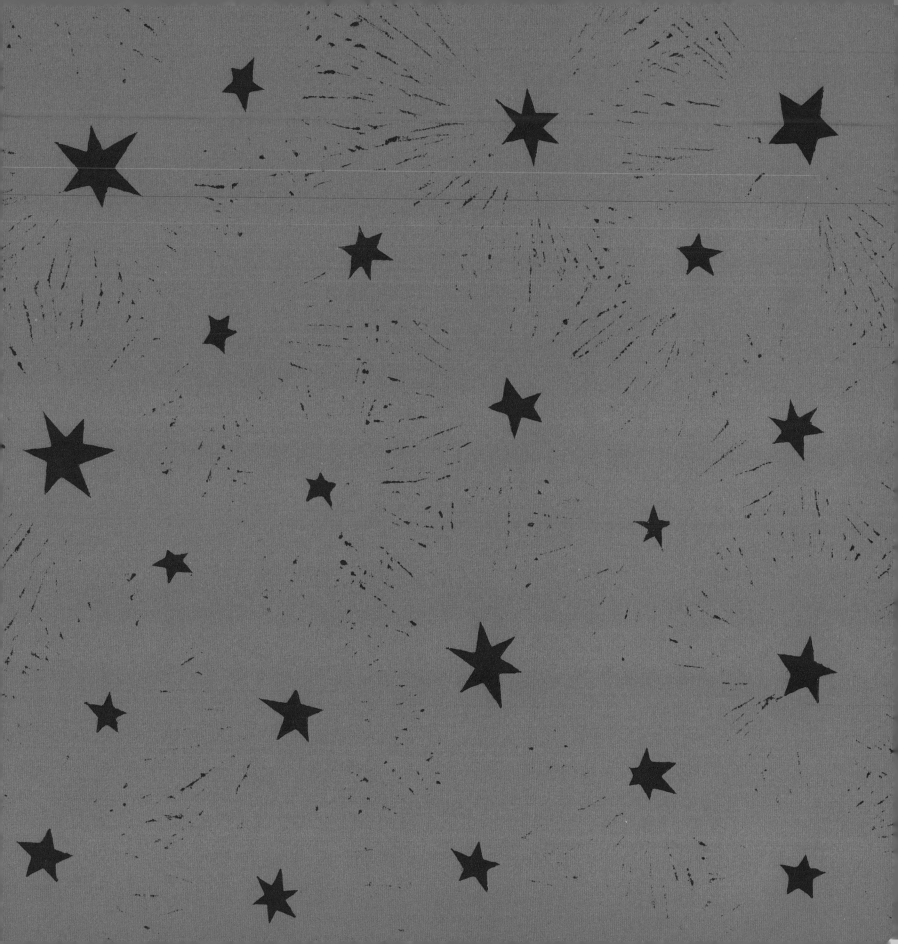

SQUARE
FISH

An Imprint of Macmillan

Square Fish and the Square Fish logo are trademarks of Macmillan and
are used by Roaring Brook Press under license from Macmillan.

Cataloging-in-Publication Data is on file at the Library of Congress
ISBN: 978-0-312-60886-6

First published in Great Britain by Macmillan Children's Books, London
Originally published in the United States by Roaring Brook Press
Square Fish logo designed by Filomena Tuosto
First Square Fish Edition: 2010
10 9 8 7 6 5 4 3 2 1
www.squarefishbooks.com

Ghosts in the House!

Kazuno Kohara

SQUARE
FISH

ROARING BROOK PRESS
NEW YORK

Once there was a girl who went to live
in a big old house at the edge of town.
It was a splendid place, but there
was one problem.

The house was . . .

...haunted!

But the girl wasn't just a girl.

She was a witch!

She knew how to catch ghosts.

"How lovely," she said.
"I hope there are some more!"

And there were.

She continued until she had caught

all the ghosts in the house.

Then she went to the kitchen . . .

. . . and put them all in the washing machine.

When they were clean she hung them out on the clothesline.

It was fine weather for drying.

After drying, most of them became nice curtains.

One of them made a good tablecloth.
They were all very useful.

The little witch began to feel very tired
after her hard work.

She knew just what to do with the last two ghosts . . .

And they all lived
happily ever after.